For Sweet Mesquite and Mrs. Fabulous
—J.S.

THIS IS A BORZOI BOOK PUBLISHED BY ALFRED A. KNOPF

Copyright © 2019 by Jennifer Sattler
All rights reserved. Published in the United States by Alfred A. Knopf,
an imprint of Random House Children's Books,
a division of Penguin Random House LLC, New York. Knopf, Borzoi Books,
and the colophon are registered trademarks of Penguin Random House LLC.

Visit us on the Web!
rhcbooks.com

Educators and librarians, for a variety of teaching tools, visit us at
RHTeachersLibrarians.com

Library of Congress Cataloging–in–Publication Data
Names: Sattler, Jennifer Gordon, author, illustrator.
Title: Dollop and Mrs. Fabulous / Jennifer Sattler.
Description: First edition. | New York : Alfred A. Knopf, 2019. | Summary:
When Dollop joins her sister, Lily, for a tea party, rules get in the way
of fun, but soon Lily's concern for manners and Dollop's ninja skills come together.
Identifiers: LCCN 2018026940 (print) | LCCN 2018033573 (ebook) |
ISBN 978-0-399-55337-0 (ebook) | ISBN 978-0-399-55335-6 (hardback) | ISBN 978-0-399-55336-3 (glb)
Subjects: | CYAC: Sisters—Fiction. | Play—Fiction. | Tea—Fiction. |
Parties—Fiction. | Etiquette—Fiction. | Rabbits—Fiction. | Humorous
stories. | BISAC: JUVENILE FICTION / Family / Siblings. | JUVENILE FICTION
/ Animals / Rabbits. | JUVENILE FICTION / Imagination & Play.
Classification: LCC PZ7.S24935 (ebook) | LCC PZ7.S24935 Dol 2019 (print) |
DDC [E]—dc23

The text of this book is set in 19-point ShagExpert-Lounge.
The illustrations were created using watercolor, pencil, colored pencil, and Photoshop.

MANUFACTURED IN CHINA
February 2019   10 9 8 7 6 5 4 3 2 1   First Edition

DOLLOP AND Mrs. Fabulous

Jennifer Sattler

Alfred A. Knopf　New York

Dollop was b-o-r-e-d.

Even her favorite toys were boring.

I'M GONNA EAT YOU!

NO, I'M GONNA EAT YOU!

She was just putting
Alfonzo in time-out when
she heard a sound from
the next room.

Oh my, Rainbow McSprinkles!
What a lovely idea!

Her sister, Lili, was up to something. But what? Dollop decided to use her ninja spy skills to find out.

It was a tea party!

"Can I play?" asked Dollop.

"I guess so," said Lili. "But there are no ninjas at tea parties."

"You have to be on your best manners. That means using a napkin."

"And raising your pinkie finger *like so* when you sip your tea."

"And you have to *dress* for a tea party, too!"

Lili got dressed for the party.

So did Dollop.

When they were ready, Lili had transformed
into Mrs. Fabulous.

While Dollop was . . . Dollop.

Mrs. Fabulous invited her best-behaved guests.

Dollop brought some friends, too.

Then it was time
to start the party.

Sugar cube?

Lemon?

GLUG

GLUG

GLUG

Dollop! Not so much!

Mrs. Fabulous was shocked.
"There's no burping at a tea party!
Let's move on to polite conversation."

Isn't the weather lovely?

Aren't the cups pretty?

Oh my, your dress is fabulous, Sweetums!

But Dollop had had enough.

Lili tried to keep the tea party going,
but somehow the mood just wasn't the same.

Meanwhile, Dollop's monsters were just
about to battle each other when suddenly . . .

Dollop! Come quick!
Sweetums is trying to
kiss Alfonzo!

Dollop leapt into action!

THERE'S NO KISSING
AT TEA PARTIES!

"Dollop! That was FABULOUS. From now on, *every* tea party needs a ninja."